VOLUME TWO

Smythe, Rachel (Comics a
Lore Olympus. Volume 2 /
[2022]
33305250316548
ca   08/03/22

LORE OLYMPUS

VOLUME TWO

RACHEL SMYTHE

DEL REY

NEW YORK

Lore Olympus: Volume Two is a work of fiction.
Names, places, characters, and incidents either are the product of
the author's imagination or are used fictitiously. Any resemblance to actual persons,
living or dead, events, or locales is entirely coincidental.

Copyright © 2022 by Rachel Smythe and WEBTOON™
All rights reserved.

Published in the United States by Del Rey, an imprint of Random House,
a division of Penguin Random House LLC, New York.

DEL REY and the HOUSE colophon are registered trademarks of Penguin Random House LLC.

Portions of this work originally appeared on Webtoons.com.

LIBRARY OF CONGRESS CATALOGING-IN-PUBLICATION DATA
Names: Smythe, Rachel (Comics artist), author, artist.
Title: Lore Olympus / Rachel Smythe.
Description: First edition. | New York : Del Rey, 2022
Identifiers: LCCN 2021008087 | Hardcover ISBN 9780593160305 (v. 2) |
Trade paperback ISBN 9780593356081 (v. 2)
Subjects: LCSH: Mythology, Greek—Comic books, strips, etc. | Graphic novels.
Classification: LCC PN6727.S54758 L67 2021 | DDC 741.5/973—dc23
LC record available at https://lccn.loc.gov/2021008087

Printed in China

Original WEBTOON editors: Bekah Caden, Annie LaHue
Rachel Smythe art assistants: Johana R. Ahumada, M. Rawlings, Court Rogers
WEBTOON translation: Anastasia Gkortsila
Penguin Random House team: Ted Allen, Erin Korenko, and Sarah Peed

randomhousebooks.com

2 4 6 8 9 7 5 3 1

First Edition

Book design by Edwin Vazquez

To Eunice Yooni Kim,
thank you for noticing me.

CONTENT WARNING
FROM RACHEL SMYTHE

Lore Olympus regularly deals with themes of physical and mental abuse, sexual trauma, and toxic relationships.

Some of the interactions in this volume may be distressing for some readers. Please exercise discretion, and seek out the support of others if you require it.

EPISODE 26

YOU CALLED

YOU ANSWERED

It's late.

Y-you called.

You answered.

You know, text messages really help if you add your name.

//////

I've never had a phone before--

Wait...

How did you work out it was me then?

Everything is different here...

Do you want to go home?

I could take you.

Persephone?

No.

I think if I went home now, I'd want to stay and not come back.

If it's any consolation, Olympus wears me the fuck out.

So you're not alone.

Really?

Really. Also the coffee there is just terrible.

SNORT

SIGH

Gods, this is embarrassing.

Stop smiling!

Oh? How can you tell?

I can hear it in your stupid voice.

Listen, I don't want to make you feel like I'm dissecting you.

When I first saw you at the party, you looked sad.

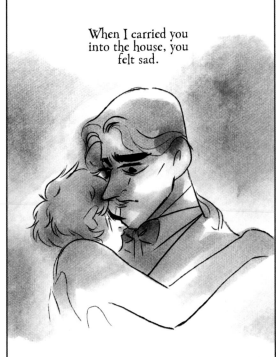

When I carried you into the house, you felt sad.

EPISODE 27: DEAL

Persephone?

Persephone?

You're important.

I didn't mean to upset you, I'm sorry--

Me? What do I have to contribute?

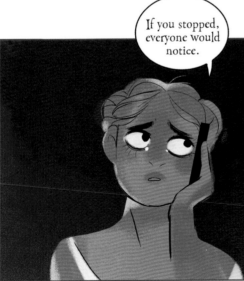

If you stopped, everyone would notice.

Flowers and junk.

My mom could manage Spring herself before I was born.

In fact, she's doing it for me right now, so I can be here.

What does that say about me and my role?

If I wasn't here, everything would be fine--

Fine is a dirty four-letter word that starts with F.

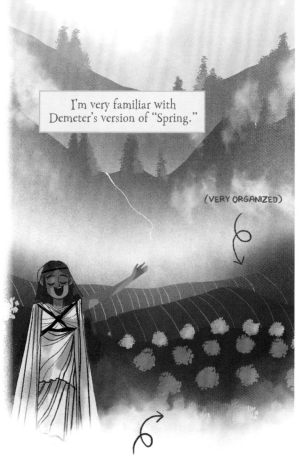

I'm very familiar with Demeter's version of "Spring."

(VERY ORGANIZED)

(NICE AND TIDY)

Spring executed by Demeter is...

...practical and straight to the point.

You could measure it with a ruler.

SNIFF

S-sure.

SLIDE

Did you... did you get to choose your job?

EPISODE 28: AWKWARD SILENCE

Then there was
Hestia.

But she took a
vow of celibacy.

I liked Hestia, but
a wife who's taken
a vow of celibacy
isn't for me.

That left Demeter.

Ever the contrarian...

Who seemed to find it necessary to argue with me about absolutely everything.

WAIT!

WAIT!

WAIT!

More stories! Less Mom stuff.

Okay, okay!

After the war ended, I was assigned to the Underworld.

And the Underworld doesn't run itself, that's for sure.

It involves a lot of long hours...

Seven-day weeks.

I got really busy and just kinda didn't want to try anymore.

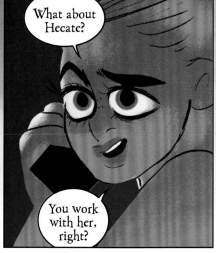
What about Hecate?

You work with her, right?

N-no.

You?

Is eternal maidenhood for you?

Doesn't that sound like fun!?

Mama, this sounds like the opposite of fun.

...I'm not seeing anyone.

RUB
RUB

I must be keeping you.

Nah, I'm normally up at this time anyway.

SIGH
Good.

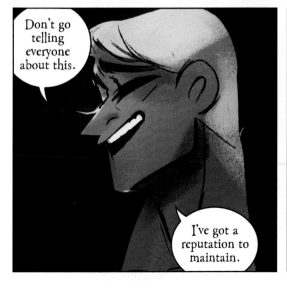

Don't go telling everyone about this.

I've got a reputation to maintain.

I won't, I promise.

HEY! CHOP-CHOP!

Come on, you know how I feel about being late.

You two have to go to daycare because you can't be trusted in the house.

PANT PANT PANT

GIGGLE

EPISODE 29: THUNDER

Would it have been so hard for you to take my side?

I know you're upset with me, but did you REALLY have to show Hades that photo?

If you want someone to blindly agree with you, go whine to your stupid little PA.

SMACK

I command you to stop!

Dammit.

Please--

Bunny, he likes her. I mean, really likes her.

And he doesn't like anyone.

...What's the harm?

You're joking, right?

The age differ--

HUFF

HUFF

HUFF

Sigh

What do you want from me, Zeus?

Since when have you been afraid of your wife's opinion?

I'm going to work.

Stop...

wait...

And we have a very special guest this morning.

But I thought you and Uncle Hades were friends?

We are...

It's just complicated, sweetheart.

Grown-up stuff.

BOOP!

I think you and Papa are just mad at each other and Hades doesn't have anything to do with it.

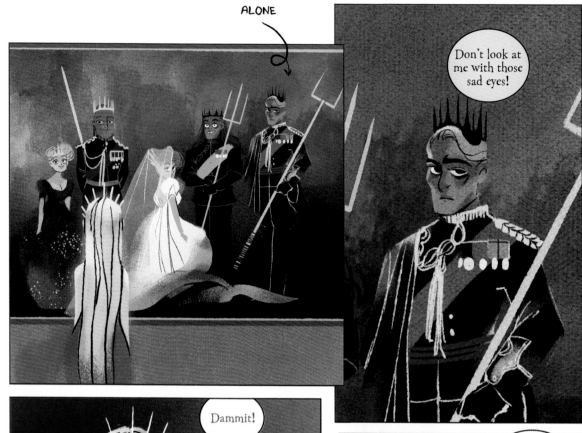

ALONE

Don't look at me with those sad eyes!

Dammit!

Does my 8-year-old have more emotional intelligence than me?

Have I been unfair to you, old friend?

I guess I have neglected him in the marriage department...

I know I shouldn't have shown Hades that picture.

But I can't take that back now.

I don't even think she likes Apollo...

She looked terrified.

Apollo
Today at 11.15am

Get to hang with this cutie today! 😊😊😊 #Blessed

SILENT PLOTTING

EPISODE 30: HERA INTERFERES

SNAP!

Did you know there is a really dorky portrait of you at Hera's? 🌑

INVOLUNTARY MOAN

...Hades, I'm in a lot of trouble.

NOT to say that they are ugly, they're still very good-looking!

Not that I think your husband is good-looking!!!

Haaa...

If this turns out to be an elaborate scheme to see Persephone's big boobs...

I'm going to kill all 3 of them.

WHAAAAATTTT!!!???

UNDERWORLD CORP

OLYMPUS TO UNDERWORLD INTERN EXCHANGE PROGRAM

APPLICANT: PERSEPHONE (KORE)

REPORT TO: HADES, GOD/KING OF THE DEAD/UNDERWORLD

LOCATION: UNDERWORLD CORP, TOWER I, LV 99

TIME: ASAP

INTERNSHIP ROLE DESCRIPTION : TO BE DISCUSSED

STATUS: APPROVED BY HERA, QUEEN OF THE GODS

PLEASE ATTACH PHOTO ID

Embarrassing
old photo.

NO.

NO.

NO.

NO.

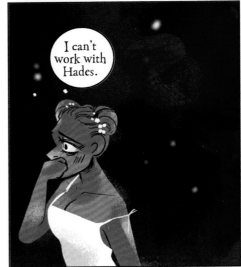

I can't work with Hades.

I told him all that personal stuff about me!

He's gonna be my boss?

EPISODE 31: A TREAT FOR BEING A FOOL

I haven't taken my vows or had a ceremony, so I'm not an official member yet.

Yeah... there is that.

OH PHEW!

...

I mean, that's so interesting, tell me more!

My mother really wants me to be like Artemis...

She's amazing, you know?

I guess, if you like unladylike belligerence.

NOPE

No interest in getting married then?

Marriage is my specialty!

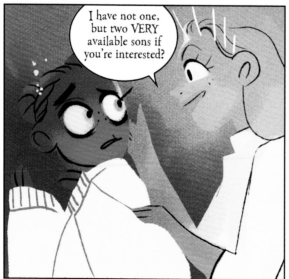

I have not one, but two VERY available sons if you're interested?

Me? Married!?

I can't say I've thought about it.

Well, if you ever change your mind, let me know.

Wouldn't you prefer to speak with him in person...

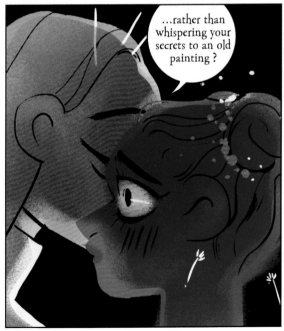

...rather than whispering your secrets to an old painting?

Um, Your Majesty?

Sorry, just lost in thought!

I'd better get going. I've got class.

YAP!
YAP!
YAP!

Listen very carefully.

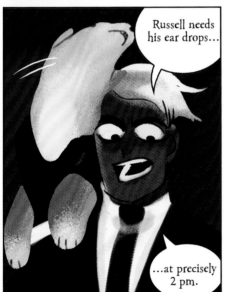

Russell needs his ear drops...

...at precisely 2 pm.

If you fail to administer his ear drops at that time,

I will know...

Sure, sure!

(TOO TALL)

(IS FINE)

EPISODE 32: SMALL

Come on, Aphrodite... we don't have anything to do with each other.

That's not the point.

You were rude.

You've never done me any favors--

It's about respect!

Respect? HUH!

You can barely stand to make eye contact with me half the time.

SIGH

Look.

If you had just wanted to punish me I would have been fine with that...

Persephone didn't do anything to you besides be there.

S-s-she got upset, you know?

Pe-Perse-Persephone could have gotten really sick.

You're stammering...

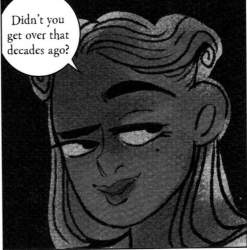

Didn't you get over that decades ago?

I have this feeling that I don't quite understand...

I really don't want anything bad to happen to her...

So from now on, I want you to leave her alone.

...

Only if you take back what you said at the party.

I could.

But it would be a lie.

...Oh for fuck's sake.

EPISODE 33: YOUR ROYAL MAJESTY

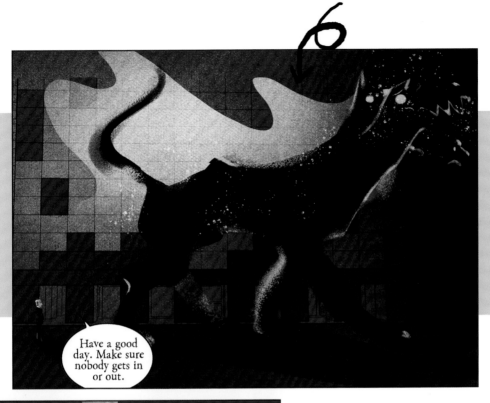

(Self-sufficient.)

Have a good day. Make sure nobody gets in or out.

Did you know there is a really dorky portrait of you at Hera's? 😬

I don't know what to reply.

Did you know there is a really dorky portrait of you at Hera's? 😬

You would make a much better subject for a painting.

Ah! Don't send her that, you idiot.

Did you know there is a really dorky portrait of you at Hera's? 💀

You would make a muc

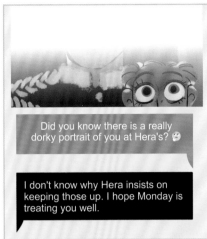

Did you know there is a really dorky portrait of you at Hera's? 💀

I don't know why Hera insists on keeping those up. I hope Monday is treating you well.

Why isn't he getting out?

TAP
TAP
TAP

Ummm, Your Majesty.

Oh.

Here.

Get your ass out of my chair.

You didn't call me back...

Or text me.

Don't tell me you're still mad--

I don't ask a lot, but you really let me down this time.

I should have been looking out for her...

Nameless flower nymph!?

Who wrote this tripe?

What?

Was that...

The Goddess of Spring, Persephone...

exiting your house?

M-maybe.

TWITCH

EPISODE 34: MIND THE GAP

SIGH

Don't look at me like that.

Let me explain.

Nothing happened. She had too much to drink. She slept in my guest room.

I drove her home in the morning.

TONK!

Would ya stop hitting me??

What have I told you about being discreet!?

This doesn't affect you in the same way.

You'll get a fucking high five at the watercooler at most.

Scholarship...?

This could put Persephone's scholarship at risk--

Wait! Do you know her!?

YOU DO!

SIGH
Remember how I took a couple of months off last year to study poisonous plants?

I stayed with Demeter in the Mortal Realm.

Persephone's been sending me letters ever since I left.

L-letters?

Do you still have them?

Can I please read them?

2000 and something-ish.

SIGH
What a mess.

Regardless, something must be done about this.

This place is really big...

Did you know there is a really dorky portrait of you at Hera's? 🤔

I don't know why Hera insists on keeping those up. I hope Monday is treating you well.

Did you know there is a really dorky portrait of you at Hera's? 🙄

I don't know why Hera insists on keeping those up. I hope Monday is treating you well.

I've got my first class today. I'm really nervous.

Text Notification

Apollo

Hey, how are you?

EPISODE 35: THE MEAL TICKET

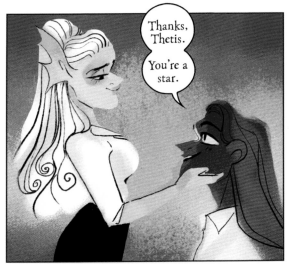

Thanks, Thetis.

You're a star.

I know.

TOSS

Time for 30 minutes of personal browsing before getting to emails...

CLICK
CLICK

It would appear your meal ticket has wandering eyes.

It's just a picture!!!

Is it though?

That smug bitch.

I don't mean to criticize, darling.

You better get your shit together, Minthe.

But I've always been skeptical about the longevity of your "treat him mean, keep him keen" approach.

I would hate to see you replaced.

Remember, don't go crying to him.

Crying is for wives.

SHE'S NOT EVEN HIS TYPE!

Artemis,
do I start
talking now?

**Yes! It's already
recording.**

*OH! Oops! Hello, Ko-- I mean,
Persephone here! I'm sorry,
I can't take your call right now.*

*Please leave a message
and I'll get back to you
as soon as I can.*

Have you heard anything from Persephone yet?

I've tried calling her but it's going to voicemail.

I'll go find her.

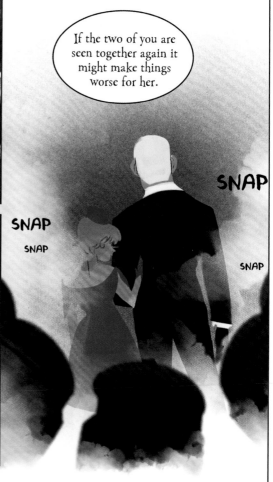

If the two of you are seen together again it might make things worse for her.

SNAP

SNAP

SNAP

SNAP

I don't think that's a good idea.

EPISODE 36: SMARTY PANTS

THUMP

You said I couldn't have that coat because you felt weird about giving away Hera's birthday present!

Yet, I see you're DELIGHTED to be giving it away to some random flower nymph with huge tits!

A flower nymph, Hades? You've got to be kidding me.

I thought you enjoyed intelligent conversation.

She looks about as smart as a baked potato.

...Are you jealous?

I'm not, I--

I thought you didn't get jealous.

Listen, it's not what it looks like. You know how the media is desperate for stories.

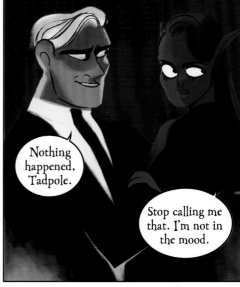

Nothing happened, Tadpole.

Stop calling me that. I'm not in the mood.

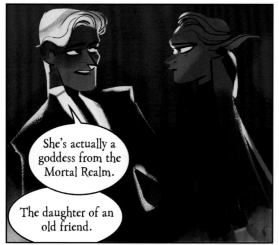

She's actually a goddess from the Mortal Realm.

The daughter of an old friend.

...Oh

Minthe.

What happened?

...

Why didn't you come to the party?

I thought we were doing so well.

This is a photo of my friend and me.

But a lot of those other statements are not true.

They must have terrible sources. *ha* How embarrassing for them.

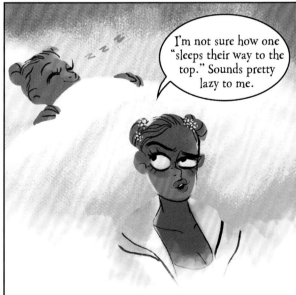

I'm not sure how one "sleeps their way to the top." Sounds pretty lazy to me.

They mean you had sex with him.

SNIFF SNIFF

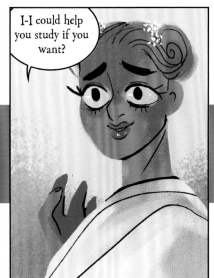

I-I could help you study if you want?

Really!?

Sit up straight, honey!

CONGRATS

1st Place

I'm behind on a lot of things in life.

NOTES

But I know I'm good at studying.

Phew, that wasn't so bad.

I'm going to get a massive lecture from Hestia...

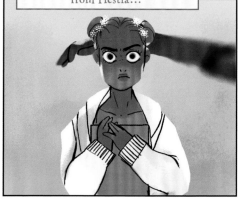

I'm not sure what I'm going to do about that article, though.

GRAB

Hey, Persie.

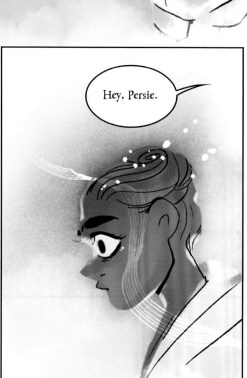

Surprise! I came to pick you up from class!

Artemis told me you'd be finished around this time.

I texted you, but you didn't text me back.

...You don't seem very surprised.

Hello, is anyone at home in there?

Apollo, what happened last night...

That can't happen again.

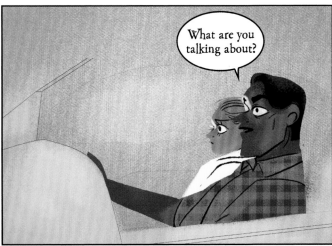
What are you talking about?

I didn't enjoy it.

O-of course you did.

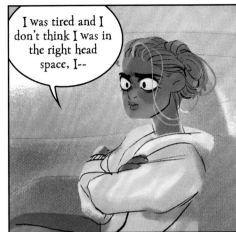

I was tired and I don't think I was in the right head space, I--

You need to relax. Look, we just need to practice.

Practice?

Artemis isn't going to be back at your place for another hour or so.

I was thinking--

EPISODE 37: A PRINCE IN DARK VELVET

BARK!

Oh no, he seems to hate you...

What should I do?

Can you grab my backpack?

It has my homework in it.

Come on. I need my backpack.

May I come in?

Certainly not. But you may continue to lurk.

Splendid one.

This life that others have planned for you--

And I suppose you have a plan for me, also?

GASP!

Another dream.

...What was that about?

EPISODE 38: MEETING READY

Ugh, I feel so nervous.

SPRITZ

It's fine, it's only Hades.

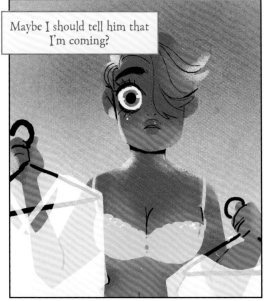

Maybe I should tell him that I'm coming?

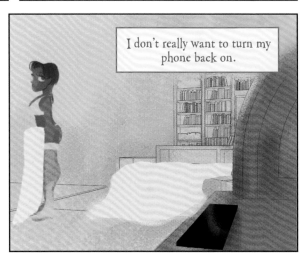

I don't really want to turn my phone back on.

I can't imagine how Apollo took yesterday.

!?

Why is he always here!?

Are you guys okay?

AHHHHHHH!

You look so cute!

I'm still not sure how I feel about you working in the Underworld, though.

What do you mean she's working in the Underworld???

That's completely inappropriate.

It's a little unorthodox, but it's Hera's direct order.

Direct orders.

Well, at the very least you could wear something more conservative in the company of Hades.

NO!

...

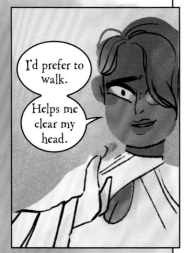

I'd prefer to walk.

Helps me clear my head.

Okay then, good luck for today.

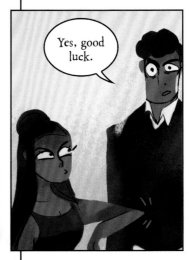

Yes, good luck.

Don't let him rattle you.

Oh my, it's very crowded.

Sorry, princess, but I'm late for my meeting.

SHOVE

Wings!?

But you've got wings!!!

Y-YOU LAZY BONES!!!

EPISODE 39: TOWER 4

Take a seat.

I read over the proposal for your salary review.

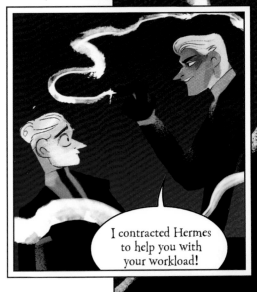

I contracted Hermes to help you with your workload!

YOU'VE BEEN LETTING YOUR PRODUCTIVITY SLIP EVER SINCE HE STARTED!

BING
BONG

Oh my...

She's so beautiful and thin.

ADJUST

Other door!

RATTLE

Wait...

Is that the girl from the article!?

What is she doing here?

Um hello, I'm supposed to meet with Hades.

And you are?

My name's Persephone.

Well, kid, you don't have an appointment.

I--

You can't just see the King of the Underworld whenever you'd like. He's very busy.

Does he have any time free today--

NO!

You didn't even look at your computer.

I don't need to.

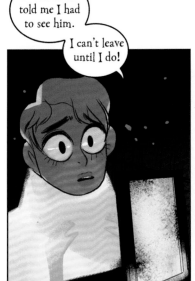

But H-Hera told me I had to see him.

I can't leave until I do!

I see...

Okay, so he's probably doing the rounds right about now.

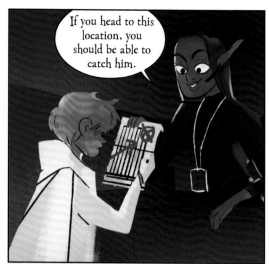

If you head to this location, you should be able to catch him.

Really? Thank you.

Ya better hurry.

Oh, oh right.

Bye!

Hehe

HUFF
HUFF

Hopefully I can hide
from them.

HERMES THANATOS

See how Hermes collected 230 souls last month.

See how your piece of the pie is reeeeally tiny?

Minthe, can you read that last part back?

THANATOS

SIGH

This is so stupid.

WHOOP!

EPISODE 40: HIDE AND SNEAK

I can reimburse you for the coat.

...But it's got a brooch my mom gave me.

And I had some paperwork with me...

If I get someone else to find those things...

will you stop worrying and come back to the office?

EPISODE 41: RETURN OF THE PRINCESS

CAMERA FEED 22

What are they--

OH!

EVERYTHING IS FINE. EVERYONE, PLEASE GET BACK TO WORK.

MASH MASH

DVD

Haaa

DVD

DVD

W-who was that girl?

You mean, "Who is that *woman?*"

I may have cut in front of her at the station this morning.

She's the daughter of a friend of Hades.

She's not just *the daughter of a friend of* Hades.

⁉

⁉

She's a descendant of the 6 Traitors Dynasty.

She's the only daughter of Demeter.

Smile pretty for the photographer, sweetheart!

And heiress to the Barley Mother fortune.

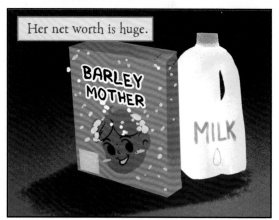

Her net worth is huge.

... And you cut in front of her at the station.

Good luck with that.

FUCK!?

THAT LITTLE
BITCH!

This is weird.

It's good to be warm again, though.

My chest feels really tight.

Maybe Eros was right?

Is this what having a crush feels like?

I wish I'd had one before so I could know I'm having one right now.

I guess it's okay not to know.

For now, I can just enjoy looking at his dorky face.

KNOCK KNOCK

Are you all right in there?

I'm f-fine, thank you!

Okay... You're just kinda accident prone.

Heh

EPISODE 42: THE WAY SHE LOOKED AT ME

Every time she's around me,
she ends up getting hurt.

But, the way she looked
at me...

No, don't be an idiot.

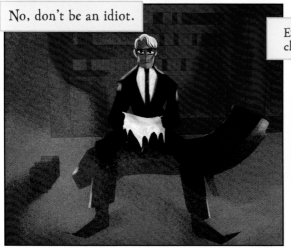

Even if there is the smallest
chance she does want me...

...she's still too young, and I'm still a complete mess.

I don't want to ruin her with my emotional bullshit. It wouldn't be fair.

The sooner she can get away from me, the better.

Um, excuse me, don't you have a gateway to guard?

I see I'm old news, huh?

Would you cut that out?

BARK! BARK! BARK! BARK!

SQUEEZE

PUSH

Oh my goodness, you're so clever! Come here. ♥

SLAM!

Get your shit together.

TAP
TAP

S-sorry for interrupting.

With all the commotion, I didn't even notice what she was wearing.

INTERNAL MOANING

MORE INTERNAL MOANING

Ugh, is it my hair? It goes frizzy when it air dries.

No, no, I was just lost in thought.

Please, take a seat.

DIG DIG

I thought you could use this for your hair.

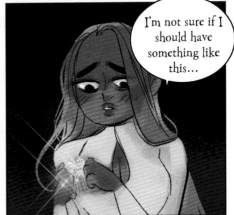

I'm not sure if I should have something like this...

Come on.

It's the least I can do after what happened this morning.

What was that place? W-who were those creatures?

That was Tartarus. It's where we keep the more problematic shades.

Typically, the ones you came across are dormant.

But they felt threatened by you since they're dead...

and you're a fertility goddess.

WHOA there, pal, I'm no fertility goddess!

OH-um-sorry, I shouldn't have assumed.

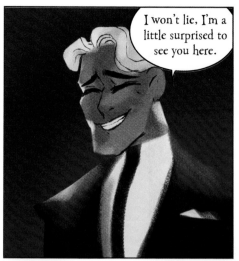

I won't lie, I'm a little surprised to see you here.

This is actually for you.

For me?
CHUCKLE

Heh...

I'm sorry, but this is out of the question.

What!? B-but why?

You were here for all of 2 seconds, and you were nearly strangled.

But that wasn't my fault! I--

I-I-I'll talk to Hera and make new arrangements for you.

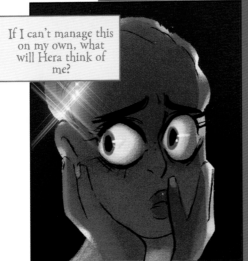

If I can't manage this on my own, what will Hera think of me?

No, but I need *this* job.

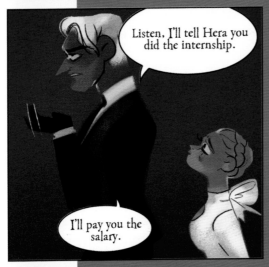

Listen, I'll tell Hera you did the internship.

I'll pay you the salary.

And you can just... do something else with your time.

I can't just not do the work.

CLICK

EPISODE 43: THE WAGER

I mean, *what a cute little castle that is!!!*

My mother says it's better if I learn how to make my own way.

And I don't disagree.

Don't get me wrong, I love her very much.

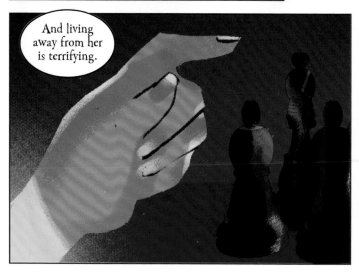
And living away from her is terrifying.

But I'm also excited to be my own person.

Is that snow?

I've never seen it before.

It's too warm in the Mortal Realm.

Can we go to the roof?

I want a better look.

No!

Are you in a perpetual state of wanting shit that's bad for you?

Please?

SHRUG

5 minutes, tops.

BARK!

I'm in trouble.

I'm in *a lot* of trouble.

We are very lucky to receive a candidate who happens to be an esteemed member of the Olympus family.

I'd like to present someone who needs no introduction but is going to get one anyway.

Give a warm welcome to our newest intern, Persephone, the Goddess of Spring.

CLAP CLAP

CLAP CLAP

...

Since when did interns receive all staff, formal introductions?

EPISODE 44: SOFT

N-no, I don't think I've had the pleasure...

TUG!

TUG!

What is she doing!? I don't get it.

This is Minthe, she's my personal assistant.

This is Pers--

Persephone. Yes, I've got it.

I should have been more careful. I'm sorry.

...

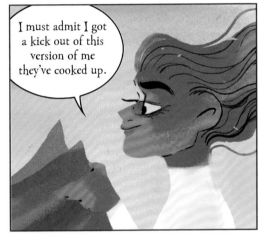

I must admit I got a kick out of this version of me they've cooked up.

SUNDAY MORNING SCANDAL

Sleeping her way to the top!

Who is the pink minx sleazing her way into the royal family?

The real thing is far less interesting...

MRRRRRRRRRR

Don't forget...
that you're my girl.

EPISODE 45: CRUSHED

Surely I can control my feelings and maintain my dignity.

PULL

She's not *that* great.

She just makes me feel all warm and snuggly inside when I think about her.

Do I even like feeling warm and snuggly?

Who does she think she is making me feel warm and snuggly!?

TUG!

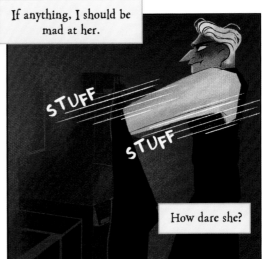

If anything, I should be mad at her.

STUFF

STUFF

How dare she?

And yet...

She's really easy to talk to and makes me forget about where I am and what I should be doing.

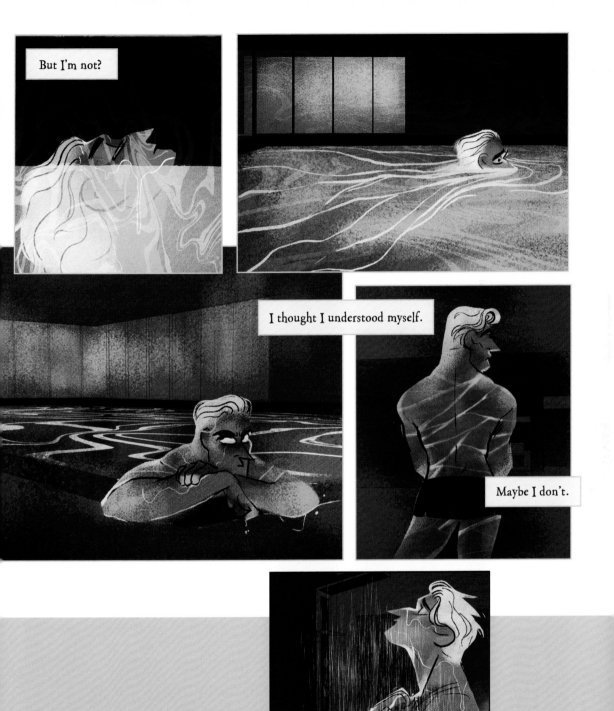

Her ass even looks like an upside down heart.

GAH!

WIPE WIPE

Why is Hera doing this to me? It must be some elaborate joke at my expense.

Your sexual frustration is so entertaining!

I can't be a 2000-year-old man with a crush on a 19-year-old.

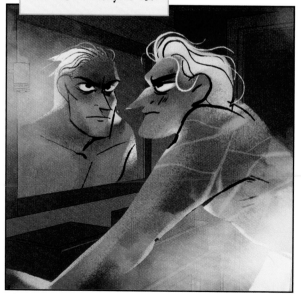

Okay, I'm going to stop having a crush on her in:

One...

Two...

Three.

How do I stop this? She's basically perfect.

But nobody is perfect...

There has to be something wrong with her.

No results, of course.

There is something on the back of her application?

Academic transcript, huh?

Let's see...

Man, what an overachiever.

✓ OVERALL WINNER CHESS OLYMPUS CHAMPIONSHIP, 3 TIMES RUNNING

✓ JUNIOR SWIMMING OLYMPIAN SWIMMING CHAMPION

✓ MATHEMATICS CHAMPION

TGOEM Scholarship?

Oh yeah, Hecate mentioned she had a scholarship.

Oracle

TGOEM

Oracle Search   I'm feeling blessed

Oracle offered in: Latin

The Goddesses of Eternal Maidenhood
Live a life devoted to the service of others.

TGOEM: LATEST NEWS | HOME | ABOUT | APP

NEWEST RECIPIENT OF THE TGOEM
ACADEMIC SCHOLARSHIP

ACADEMIC
SCHOLARSHIP

SLAM!

And I asked her if she was a fertility goddess.

I'm such a fucking moron!

Did I misread this whole situation?

KNOCK KNOCK KNOCK

!?

4 DAYS AGO!
(THE DAY OF THE PARTY)

Man, I need a smoke!

Where's my lighter?

Hades must have a lighter somewhere...

Huh?

DIG

EPISODE 46: RED RAW

A

B

C

Why is he doing this?

Zeus & Hera cordially invite you to

The 1500th Panathenaea!

Where: 467 Gigantomachy Crescent
When: 8pm

This invitation is for Minthe.

We both agreed that neither of us are relationship material.

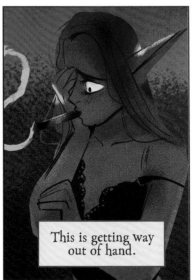

This is getting way out of hand.

We're not even in a public relationship on Fatesbook!

How can he be considering marriage!?

CLICK CLICK

I can't be queen.

CLICK CLICK

It's too much pressure.

PRESENT DAY

I DON'T CARE!
I DON'T CARE!
I DON'T CARE!

It's not like we're exclusive. He's not my boyfriend or anything.

I didn't want to marry him, why do I care!?

Why do I feel jealous?

...Don't panic, even if he starts dating her, it doesn't mean what we have is over.

Unless...

Maybe she'll want all of him to herself.

And maybe he'd like that...

HUFF
HUFF
HUFF

I thought we were supposed to be messed up together?

And now you get to be all normal and well-adjusted with her?

P-please, Hades, please don't leave me behind.

I don't know what we have, but I'm not ready for it to be over.

EPISODE 47: NEEDED

My therapist assigned me the exercise of writing letters of what I would hypothetically tell others about what I'm feeling.

Dear Persephone,

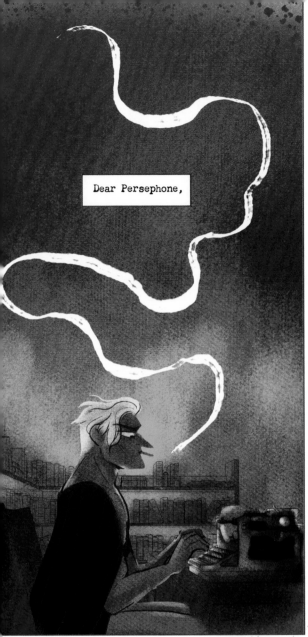

Apparently doing this will help me "UNPACK MY EMOTIONS AND GAIN A GREATER UNDERSTANDING OF MYSELF."

Gods, why do I pay that hack?

Luckily I never have to show anybody these letters so I guess it doesn't hurt to try.

This feels ridiculous to admit, given that I've only known you for 4 days.

But...
I have feelings for you.

I haven't been in love before.

I always assumed that being in love would be something that would happen slowly over time...

...not all at once.

The thing is,
I don't really know you.

I don't know what your favorite food is or the top ten things you hate.

I don't know if you're a morning person or if you like sleeping in for hours...

Love isn't something I know a lot about...

The concept of not being able to feel that way again is devastating.

I have a lot of shame in regard to feeling like this about you.

That's a lot to put on someone who is so young.

It goes without saying, I have a lot of baggage.

I get the feeling that if we were friends...

...you would go out of your way to help me.

Even if it was to your own detriment.

I wouldn't want that for you.

SUNDAY MORNING SCANDAL

SOURCES SAY A NAMELESS FLOWER NYMPH WAS SEEN LEAVING THE KING OF THE UNDERWORLD'S TOWNHOUSE, EARLY SUNDAY MORNING.

The best gift I can give you is to put some space between us.

Which is why I'm going to give Minthe and me a chance to be in a proper relationship.

I don't know if I want her or if I just feel guilty.

SUNDAY MORNING SCANDAL!
Sleeping her way to the top!
Who is the
minx

The difference between you and her is that she needs me.

But you don't.

You have your own community.

People who care for you and have your best interests in mind.

You have your own goals...

Your own life.

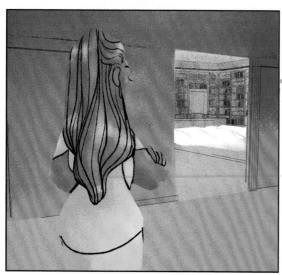

I said that you were melancholic.

This is still the case, but I can tell that you're tough as well.

If you're the daughter of Demeter, you'll be tough.

I wish I could empty a drawer in my dresser for you.

Or buy you a toothbrush to keep in my bathroom.

The truth is, every time we have something to do with each other...

it ends up hurting you.

Ultimately, you're better off if I limit my contact with you.

Which will be hard, since I'm your boss now.

But I'll try my best to keep you safe in my own way.

All the best,
Hades.

PS: How does a goddess go
from being called Kore to
Persephone?

I still feel like garbage!!!

That's what I get for trusting my therapist.

Into the drawer you go.

EPISODE 48: SISSSS

SOB!

IT SHOULD HAVE BEEN ME!

Sleeping her way to the top

Who is tʰ

~~lilac~~ ~~ni~~ mi

sleazing h

way into tʰ

royal famil

I HAVE PROOF! FACTS! DOC-U-MEN-TA-TION!

You need to stop it with that book!

You just have it on you!?

I'm sorry, but I just don't think Hades is into you.

AH-

CHU!

BLEH.

Excuse me.

COMPLETELY DELUSIONAL

He gave me all these signals and I thought we really had something going on.

Megaera, those are not signals.

Shhhh, that's our mark.

Yup, that's the photographer.

Now, remember, don't hurt him...

Just rough 'im
up a little.

Morning, Alex.

Hey, Tori.

I really wanted to ask my roommate if he was responsible for that article...

Have-have a nice day.

Will do.

EPISODE 49: EYE FOR AN EYE

So...

...Minthe.

That's an interesting turn of events.

You know already?

Please, I know everything.

Plus Minthe put it on Fatesbook.

I thought you'd be happy with my decision.

Shall we get started?

Sure!

Salutations, I'm Hecate.

My client and I would like to speak with you in regard to your crimes against the Underworld.

C-crimes!?

NUMBER 1. Defamation of character.

I don't know if you realize this, but that nymph isn't a nymph, she's a goddess.

Not only that, she's one of the Goddesses of Eternal Maidenhood.

So your garbage-shaped publication could be rather damaging for her.

This chapter takes place before Persephone's coat was confiscated by Hestia.

I was initially planning to include this, but I was unable to structure in the concept at the time. In some ways I think that contextualizing Hestia's seemingly cruel behavior takes away from the emotional impact of episode 47, "Needed," which to this day, is one of my favorite pieces of work.

With all that being said, part of me still really wants the readers of *Lore Olympus* to know this missing part of the story.

Edited by Kathleen Wisneski
Art Assistants Jaki Haboon & Amy Kim

It's all coming together. There will be spaces to rent for events.

And a range of free classes--

That all sounds fantastic.

And we've got a new initiate to the group, which is great to finally get the ball rolling.

Persephone will make such a great addition.

Persephone, you say?

Yeah.

...What is it?

Well, gosh, Hestia, I don't know if it's my place to say.

Well, now you have to tell me!

It's just that...

ABOUT THE AUTHOR

RACHEL SMYTHE is the creator of the Eisner-nominated *Lore Olympus*, published via WEBTOON.

Twitter: @used_bandaid

Instagram: @usedbandaid

Facebook.com/Usedbandaidillustration

LoreOlympusBooks.com